DISNEY PRESENTS A PIXAR FILM

THE INCREDIBLES

Never Wear a Cape!

And Other Tips for Supers

A STEPPING STONE BOOK™

Random House 🏠 New York

Library of Congress Control Number: 2004101373

ISBN: 0-7364-2267-6

www.randomhouse.com/kids/disney

Printed in the United States of America

10 9 8 7 6 5 4 3 2 1

DISNEP PRESENTS A PIXAR FILM

THE INCREDIBLES

Never Wear a Cape!

And Other Tips for Supers

by Mr. Incredible
as told to Jasmine Jones

Illustrated by Scott Caple
Designed by Winnie Ho of Disney Publishing's Global Design Group
Inspired by the art and character designs created by
Pixar Animation Studios

INTRODUCTION

Greetings, fellow Supers!

Please note: the information in this book is confidential and is not intended for those without Super powers. It would be considered hazardous for normal citizens to read this book, just as it would be hazardous for them to try to leap over buildings or run on water. It won't work, and you run the risk of injuring yourself or others. If you are unsure whether you are a Super, PLEASE ASK YOURSELF THE FOLLOWING QUESTIONS BEFORE READING ANY FURTHER:

- Can I lift two tons without breaking a sweat?
- Can I turn moisture in the air into ice?
- Can I stretch across a four-lane city street to catch a crook?
- Have I demonstrated any other such amazing abilities?

Okay, so you think you are a Super? Good.

As you know, we're back, and we're ready for action. We've been in hiding far too long. This book is for those of you who got a little rusty during the undercover years as much as it is for those of you who are just starting your hero careers. So pay attention. There is still a lot of saving to do in the world. Now let's get started. We'll start with a little history—the time that we Supers like to call the glory days.

CHAPTER 1

History of Supers

Fifteen years ago, Supers were at the top of their game. As a group, we Supers protected good citizens everywhere from the plots of evil villains, as well as from unfortunate accidents. There was always a lot to be done. Still, no matter how many times we saved the world, there was always another catastrophe on the horizon. We were always needed, and we were always ready to rescue. Those were the glory days of heroes.

Now, I know I have had a reputation for living in the past, trying too hard to relive the glamorous heroics of my youth, but they really were good times.

I remember once, I managed to make two great saves at the same time. I was driving down the street when the radio announced that there was a high-speed chase between police and gunmen happening nearby. I locked their location into the Incredibile—my amazing car—and took off after them to help. But I had just managed to change into my Super suit when an older woman flagged me down. She was obviously in need of assistance.

Her cat, Squeaker, was stuck in a tree.

My Incredibile video monitor told me that the car chase was headed my way. Of course I immediately advised the woman to step aside. You never want an innocent citizen to be hurt.

I saw the tree as the key to my success in this situation. I pulled it out of the ground and shook the cat loose, completing my first rescue. With Squeaker settled safely in his owner's arms, I lifted the tree and slammed it down in the road just in time for the crooks' car to barrel right into it. That stopped them right in their tracks.

I then replanted the tree, of course.

I can't take all the credit for that save. Without the Incredibile's tracking device, my timing could have been off, and that double save could have been a double miss. The Incredibile was extremely useful in many different crime-fighting situations. Not only that, but I looked really good in that car.

The Incredibile*

Here are some of the features of my Incredibile:

Hood emblem: glowed with the press of a button. **Cool.**

Windshield: bulletproof, fireproof, crushproof, bombproof, rocketproof glass. And it was tinted.

Auto-drive feature: could drive the car while I did other things—like change into my Super suit.

*Pictured without the roof to show the car's high-tech interior

The radio: capable of locating criminals anywhere within a hundred miles.

A regular wax job kept the Incredibile looking sleek.

Ejector button: helped me escape if I encountered something that could destroy my car (highly improbable) . . . or get rid of unwanted company.

Turbo rocket: useful for many high-speed chases.

Turn the page for the best part.

You see, the best part about a prime vehicle like the Incredibile is that I felt safe going anywhere—whether chasing criminals or saving innocent civilians. Now, that was thanks to the special all-terrain drive. Check out this picture of me in the Incredibile, saving a couple of kids who had gotten stuck on the side of a mountain. Man, I loved that car.

Super Relocation Program

Soon after the Super save with Squeaker and his owner, I was sued. Yeah, I saved a guy who apparently did not want to be saved. More lawsuits followed, and the government lost millions of dollars in court cases. That's when they started up the Super Relocation Program (SRP). All Supers, including me, went underground. And we were no longer doing hero work.

We always had secret identities, even before the start of the SRP. (Who wanted the pressure of being Super all the time?) But now, our secret identities were our only identities. It was the end of a great era, but let me assure you, it was not the end of Supers. Over time, we came out of hiding. In fact, we later saved the city of Metroville from near destruction (see Chapter 7).

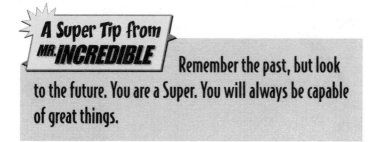

A Super Tip from MR. INCREDIBLE Remember the past, but look to the future. You are a Super. You will always be capable of great things.

Super Career Choices

Know Your Super Talent

The first and most important part of being a Super is knowing and understanding your special Super power. Lots of young Supers want to be everything to everybody when they first start out. But in fact, Supers can save many more lives simply by sticking to their talents. Stretchy Supers are not as fast as speedy Supers, and they should not pretend that they are. Of course, my wife, Elastigirl, sometimes races my Super-speedy son, Dash—but that's just for fun.

Examples of Supers Who Didn't Realize Their Own Strength

• The Super with laser vision powers who bored a hole to China while trying to save a cat trapped in a well.

• The Super with incredible strength who helped his neighbor move an oak tree but also uprooted the line to her septic tank. P.U.!

A Super Tip from MR. INCREDIBLE Never try to be a hero before you've sharpened your Super talent. It is unique. Use it wisely.

Here Is a List of Some Super Powers

• **Super transforming:** Do things freeze or melt when you touch them? If so, you're like my best buddy, Frozone. He can turn moisture into ice. Lots of Supers have the ability to make solid matter change or become invisible. This can be very useful when you need to freeze a villain in his tracks.

• *Super strength:* Do you bust through walls when you're not watching where you're going? Have you ever sawed through the table while cutting a steak? Super strength may cause problems at home, but it's great for defeating villains.

• **Super vision:** Do things disappear in a puff of smoke when you look at them? Can you see through solid objects? If so, you have Super vision powers. This can be helpful for burning through steel bars, tracking a villain, or simply heating up leftovers.

• **_Super speed:_** If high-speed vehicles with afterburners are the only things that can keep up with you, your power is Super speed! It's the perfect Super power for rushing innocent civilians from a burning building, stopping a runaway bus, and nabbing an escaped convict—and that's just on your way to lunch!

• **_Super flexibility:_** If you can touch someone standing fifty yards away or shape your body into a parachute, life raft, or rope ladder, you obviously have Super stretch powers. Anyone would love to have someone as flexible as you on his or her team. And you're one Super who will never get bent out of shape—unless it's on purpose.

• **Super invisibility:** The ability to turn invisible is a terrific power. Invisible Supers can spy on villains, sneak into hideouts, and ambush guards. It's also extremely difficult for a bad guy to use his newest death ray on you!

⬧ New Super Power?

Basically, we're always discovering new Supers with different types of abilities. If your Super power isn't listed here, let us know. We like to keep track of the Super powers out there. You never know when your special power will be needed.

A Super Tip from MR. INCREDIBLE It's important to identify and hone your special Super power, but it's even more important to be able to think on your feet in any situation.

⬧ Using Your Super Crime Sense

All Supers have a crime sense, but many don't even know it. It's extremely important for all of us Supers to practice using our crime sense. It could mean the difference between making a great save and driving by a bank robbery.

In order to sense a crime in progress, you have to slow down, concentrate, and focus your energy on picking up what I like to call villain vibes. Once you get the hang of it, you'll love it.

A Super Tip from
MR. INCREDIBLE

Sharpened Crime Sense Is Good
- It helps you know when a crime is occurring.
- It helps you spot a criminal in disguise.
- It helps you be first to arrive at a crime scene

Unsharpened Crime Sense Is Bad

It prevents you from distinguishing between big disasters and little ones. You may end up putting out someone's barbecue while there's a raging forest fire a mile away. Or you could travel to New Mexico to stop a carjacking in New York.

Undercover

Secrecy, Safety, and Seeming Normal

Your secret identity is your most valuable possession. Protect it.

This is a safety issue, folks. If villains know you're a Super, it's easy for them to take you by surprise—which can also endanger the innocent civilians living in your neighborhood. We need to protect not only ourselves, but also our families and neighbors. So please, know how to stay undercover!

A Super Tip from MR. INCREDIBLE Always carry some sort of mask with you. If you must perform a heroic act on the spur of the moment, wear it! It will quickly hide your identity.

Undercover Dos and Don'ts

• **Do** keep a mask handy when going out in public.	• **Don't** wear see-through shirts that reveal your Super suit under your normal clothes.
• **Do** wear normal clothes when out in public. As E would say, "No capes!"	• **Don't** make any unusual Super movements that might reveal your Super powers.

Blending In

Naturally, maintaining a secret identity requires you to blend in. Yes, it can be frustrating at the grocery store if you cannot reach that jar of pickles on the top shelf. But it is extremely important to follow the rules. Do not use your Super flexibility to stretch your arm those extra three feet. Do not bounce the jar off the shelf with your laser vision. You will be noticed, and then you and your family will need to be relocated.

Don't risk getting caught.

MR. iNCREDIBLE REMEMBERS:

A Close Call

During the time when Supers were underground, I got a little ambitious and started doing some secret hero work. Our wives thought we were bowling, but Frozone and I used to go out and listen to his police scanner to find out what was going on in the city.

One night we heard a call about a building
that was burning nearby. We pulled on ski
masks to protect our identities and headed
over to make some saves.

Once we got into the building, Frozone and I managed to gather a bunch of folks in need of rescue. That's when the trouble started. Frozone was dehydrated, so he couldn't freeze anything or put out the fire. We got trapped in the building. I had no choice. I busted through a brick wall.

Unfortunately, the wall belonged to a jewelry store, and the alarm went off. Frozone and I were still wearing our ski masks! We looked like criminals.

Luckily, there was a watercooler nearby. Frozone got a drink and froze the police officer. Then we escaped.

A Super Tip from MR. INCREDIBLE Doing hero work in anything but your Super suit can be risky. Don't try it unless lives are in danger.

Jobs

A day job is an excellent way to keep your identity secret. You will also be saving the world a little bit each day, even if you're not acting as an official Super. (Please contact the SRP for more career advice.)

MR. INCREDIBLE REMEMBERS:

Everyday Heroics

My last undercover job was at Insuricare. I didn't love it. But I found that I could still make a difference without using my Super skills. I brought in coffee and donuts for the office now and then. I made my own copies instead of asking the secretary to do it. And I helped people get the money Insuricare owed them from their insurance claims. It was not as exciting as saving people from a sinking ship, but I managed to put a few smiles on people's faces. And I stayed awake on the job while maintaining my secret identity . . . most of the time.

A Super Tip from MR. INCREDIBLE

Make little saves every day.

MR. INCREDIBLE REMEMBERS:

Turning "Oops!" into "Ow!"

Once, when we first moved to one of our undercover homes in the suburbs, Helen and I decided to have a backyard barbecue—you know, just to try to blend in with the rest of the populace the way the SRP wanted us to. It started out as a pretty good party. Helen and I were really trying hard. Helen didn't stretch at all. I resisted carrying more than one bag of ice outside at a time. We were feeling good.

Then one of our neighbors started talking to Helen about her career. Of course, Helen couldn't talk about who she really was. Anyway, I got a bit distracted, and before I knew it, I accidentally cut my hand with a knife. Actually, the knife was hurt more than I was—it was crushed into the shape of my knuckles. But I had to pretend I was injured or I would have been discovered. Quickly, Helen grabbed the ketchup and poured it on my hand, while I yelled, pretending to be in pain. Then Helen rushed me to her car. She shouted back to our friends that we were going to the hospital. It was a close call, but no one figured it out.

A Super Tip from MR. INCREDIBLE Keep ketchup and plenty of bandages available to help fake injuries when needed.

Family

Your Greatest Adventure

Your family is your greatest adventure. This can be difficult for some Supers to realize. I was really late for my own wedding because I couldn't see beyond my role as Mr. Incredible.

A Super-Exciting Day

You know, I have to admit, I thought being a family man would be a piece of cake for a Super like me. I mean, I had already saved dozens of citizens, and that was usually just in a day's work. But now I understand that I really undervalued the importance of family from the start. I couldn't even make it to my own wedding on time. Luckily, Helen forgave me, and she taught me a lesson that day.

It was late afternoon, and after a long day of crime-fighting, I was ready to get

married. That's when I stumbled upon Bomb
Voyage, the notorious bank robber—in the
middle of a robbery! I knew I was late, but I
had to catch the guy! Then that kid Buddy
showed up. Telling me he wanted to be my
sidekick, he flew out the window to get help.
He was using these rocket boots he had
invented. To make matters worse, Buddy
didn't realize that Bomb Voyage had clipped
a bomb to his "Incrediboy" cape.

Now I was really going to be late to the wedding, but I had to save the kid. I jumped out the window and grabbed Buddy's cape. The bomb fell, and I followed it. It exploded on some train tracks just as a train was headed toward the gaping hole. Of course, I saved the train, too.

I sped to the church, but I was really late. Helen was waiting for me. That's when I learned the first lesson about family.

"I love you," Helen whispered as we were exchanging our vows, "but if we're going to make this work, you've got to be more than Mr. Incredible."

She was right. When I went undercover, I had to be the husband and, later, the dad. And at first, I didn't do a very good job. I didn't pay enough attention to my family. I really wanted to be Super again, to relive the glory days. It wasn't until I almost lost my family that I realized that Helen and the kids are my most important job.

A Super Tip from MR. INCREDIBLE Don't get so caught up in the glory part of being Super that you neglect your family. My family is my greatest adventure.

🔴 Dealing with Super Kids

My family really is great. Helen and I now
have three Super kids. That's right. They're all
Supers. Violet, our oldest, can turn invisible
and generate force fields. Dash is Super fast.
And Jack-Jack—well, we're not sure about
the little guy right now, but he's certainly
good at making a Super mess at dinner.

Still, having Super kids can be tough. They
don't understand why they have powers, and
they don't understand why they can't use
them. When Supers were deep undercover,
it was frustrating for us adults to hide our
powers. But it was even more difficult for
Super kids who had never experienced being
Super in public.

41

How to Tell If Your Baby Has Super Powers

- You find burned holes in your baby's rubber duckies.
- Your baby twirls you in the air.
- Your baby picks up the refrigerator to ask for a bottle of milk.
- Your baby flies over the dinner table.
- Your baby stretches from his crib to the kitchen to get your attention.

MR. INCREDIBLE REMEMBERS:

Behavior Problems with Super Kids

Once, my son Dash decided to play a prank on his teacher, Mr. Kropp. When Mr. Kropp got out of his seat, Dash zoomed to his teacher's desk, dropped some tacks on his chair, and then zoomed back to his desk in a flash. There was only one problem—Mr. Kropp had hidden a video camera in the classroom. He took the video to Dash's principal. Luckily, Dash had been moving so fast that you couldn't even see him. Still, he risked blowing our cover with his little prank.

Helen and I had a long conversation about the incident. I have to admit I was proud of Dash. I mean, the kid had moved so fast that he hadn't even been caught on tape! But Helen was much more practical than I was. She reminded me that my eagerness to relive my *own* glory days was preventing me from being a good dad. It also led me to risk my family's undercover status by encouraging Dash to act out.

We talked about it, and Dash has learned to find positive ways to use his Super speed—*without* risking his undercover identity.

My daughter, Violet, had the opposite problem. She wanted to be normal so badly that she never showed her powers—except when she turned invisible! While most girls might just blush when they try to talk to a guy, Vi used her Super powers to turn absolutely invisible. But that was risky, too. What if a villain had gotten a tip as to where we were living at the time? If he had been watching the neighborhood for any signs of Super-ness, he might have caught Vi turning invisible every time a teenage guy walked by her.

Luckily, now that Dash and Vi have found an outlet for their powers by doing a little hero work, they've discovered a balance between being Super and living undercover. Violet is becoming more confident, and Dash has a large collection of second-place trophies from his school's track team.

A Super Tip from
MR. INCREDIBLE Help your Super kids find positive outlets for their amazing abilities.

Super Suits

Suave, Sophisticated, and Stretchy

Written by Edna Mode, on Special Assignment

Mr. Incredible begged me to write this section for him. He said you Supers simply *had* to have my advice. I could not refuse. So you think you need a Super suit, do you? It is not easy designing for Supers, darling. Fun—of course—but challenging. The work can consume you. I spend hours in my lab.

So you want to know about fashion? You could not have come to a better place, darling!
Megamesh
by E

You would think I would have retired after I invented megamesh. I came across it one day while playing around with titanium-bonded hyperalloy polymer threads and elastics. Megamesh was sturdy, kept its shape, and came in the most fabulous colors.

But why am I dwelling on the past? I will not even touch the stuff anymore. It can rip far too easily if, say, one is being attacked by an atomic-powered fifty-foot robot. And the dry-cleaning bills. Simply too much!

I love designing for Supers because Super suits are all about color. When Mr. Incredible showed up on my doorstep, I knew he was ready for something dramatic! His old colors were blue and black. *Blech!* So dull. The new Mr. Incredible was bold—a Super no longer content with being underground. He needed something that shouted, "I am a hero! Hear me roar!" Strong enough to withstand high explosives, yet silky and smooth. And machine washable!

49

Robert begged me to come up with suit designs for his entire family. I told him no, of course. I was far too busy, and his family's Super powers were too diverse. Perhaps if I had several years for research and the time for testing, maybe . . . but no! He wanted them right away!

I was unable to resist. I chose red and yellow with a touch of black.

I decided to start small and work up. First, the baby, Jack-Jack. It was a challenge to design for a Super so young. You know how babies are always getting into scrapes, crawling off, and—darling, face it—spitting up on themselves. *Blech!* And I had no idea what powers the baby possessed. I had to keep every precaution in mind.

Of course the suit must be completely bulletproof and withstand temperatures of over one thousand degrees—yet not chafe a baby's sensitive skin.

Next, I tackled the boy's suit. Dash can run at extremely high speeds. Naturally, when he's traveling that fast, friction can make the suit very hot, so in addition to being heat-resistant, the fabric had to breathe, and it had to be durable. I finally came up with the perfect material, which would stay cool no matter how fast the boy ran. And the boots! Darling, the grip, the traction, the sturdy soles . . . they are amazing!

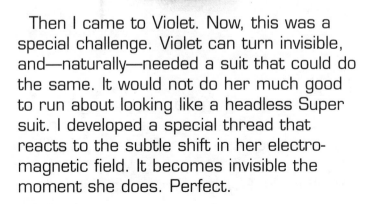

Then I came to Violet. Now, this was a special challenge. Violet can turn invisible, and—naturally—needed a suit that could do the same. It would not do her much good to run about looking like a headless Super suit. I developed a special thread that reacts to the subtle shift in her electromagnetic field. It becomes invisible the moment she does. Perfect.

Now, I have known Elastigirl for ages. For her, I developed a new elastic fabric that stretches as far as she can and still snaps right back into place. This suit breathes like Egyptian cotton. It is divine.

I would not dream of letting a normal citizen touch fabric like this. Indestructible clothing is pointless for most people, anyway. Think of the horror of having to see last year's fashions in your closet forever. Terrible!

There is one new feature that ALL the Supers will thank me for. Each suit has a homing device that sends out a signal with the wearer's precise location at the touch of a button. Elastigirl used this to find Mr. Incredible when he was trapped by that silly caped villain Syndrome. I handed her the remote and told her to try it. "Push the button, darling," I said.

It was lucky she did, because Mr. Incredible was in trouble. She immediately ran off to rescue him.

I hear the children loved their suits, which performed perfectly while they were busy saving their father. But, of course, I designed them that way, darling.

One final note: Supers, especially the men, always seem to want a cape. I have two words for these Supers: **NO CAPES!** Not only are they silly, but they are also, quite simply, dangerous. Just look at the facts, darling. I tell you, I will not even wear a scarf anymore.

Super Name	Cape?	Mishap
Thunderhead	Yes	Cape snagged on missile fin
Stratogale	Yes	Cape caught in jet turbine
Metaman	Yes	Cape tangled in express elevator cables
Splashdown	Yes	Cape sucked into vortex

There. I am done. A fabulous chapter . . . but don't even think of asking me to make you a suit. Oh well . . . if you insist.

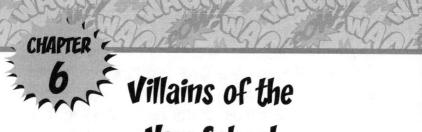

CHAPTER 6

Villains of the New School

Smarter, Slimier, Sneakier

It used to be that a villain like Bomb Voyage would just blow a hole in a jewelry store and grab a bunch of diamonds. Pretty straight-forward stuff. Mostly about getting rich quick.

Now we have villains with high-tech gizmos: robots, computers, lasers, supersonic jets—you name it. It's part of a modern Super's job to keep up with these new-age villains.

WANTED
BOMB VOYAGE

If you feel you're in trouble, behind on new technology, or simply not understanding a villain, consult your local chapter of the Supers' support group. What you don't know can and WILL hurt you.

Villain Gadgets: Cheating Their Way to World Domination

Never underestimate a villain. Syndrome didn't have any Super abilities, but he did have brains, so he made some pretty amazing stuff. Here are a few of the devices he invented:

Message Communicator

This small computer showed up in my briefcase one night. It scanned the room to see if anyone was with me. Then the face of Syndrome's assistant, Mirage, popped up. That's how they lured me back into Super work.

Jets

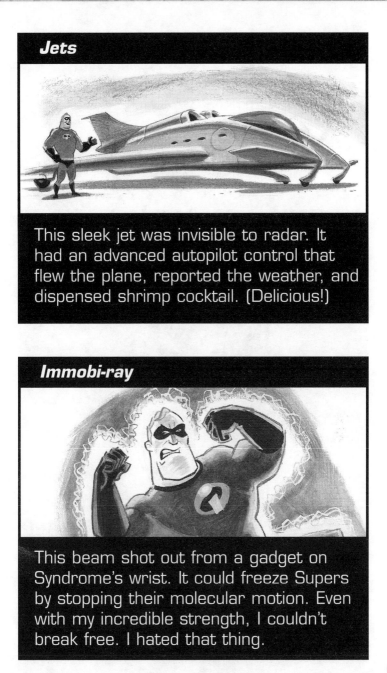

This sleek jet was invisible to radar. It had an advanced autopilot control that flew the plane, reported the weather, and dispensed shrimp cocktail. (Delicious!)

Immobi-ray

This beam shot out from a gadget on Syndrome's wrist. It could freeze Supers by stopping their molecular motion. Even with my incredible strength, I couldn't break free. I hated that thing.

Spotting Villains of the New School

Villains are getting harder to spot every day. When you're out there trying to save the world, you do not—I repeat, *do not*—want to get confused over whether someone's a Super or a villain. Villains can look like regular people—just like Supers when we're undercover.

Besides using your crime sense, here are a few tips to help you spot a villain:

• A villain's name has something negative in it, like the "bomb" in Bomb Voyage and the "ruthless" in Baroness Von Ruthless.

• Villains like to laugh evilly. Usually it sounds something like, "Moo-hoo-wah-hah-hah-hah-hah!" or "Enh-heh-heh-heh-heh-heh!"

• Villains talk a lot. We Supers call it "monologuing." They'll be right in the middle of defeating you, and suddenly they'll start talking about the brilliance of their evil plans or how powerful they are and how pathetic you are compared to them—as if anyone is really listening.

A Super Tip from MR. INCREDIBLE

Monologuing provides a great chance for escape if a villain has you trapped. Usually the villains are so interested in talking about themselves, they won't notice you getting away.

Vicious Villain Trickery

Remember Buddy with his rocket boots? He grew up to become Syndrome, one of the worst villains of all time. And he hated me for not letting him be my sidekick.

After years of plotting and planning, Syndrome tricked me into working for him. He built a learning robot, the Omnidroid. Then he brought me to his jungle island and had me defeat the robot using my Super powers. He had Mirage tell me that I was working for the government. Afterward, Syndrome rebuilt and reprogrammed the Omnidroid so that it could defeat me! That was embarrassing. I should have known.

Only later did I discover that he had done the exact same thing to dozens of my Super friends. None of them had survived.

Syndrome's plan was to get rid of all the Supers (including Helen and me!). Then he wanted to send the Omnidroid to Metroville. After the Omnidroid scared everyone, Syndrome would show up, fight the robot, and use his remote control to stop it—and make himself look like a Super. What a fraud! But we taught him a lesson. (Refer to Chapter 7 for more on this.)

A Super Tip from **MR. INCREDIBLE** There's a big difference between an adoring fan and a fan who's gone over the edge. Beware of fans who seem too eager.

Teamwork

Being a Super is great. And each Super's power is a force in its own right. But remember, never underestimate the power of teamwork.

I used to work alone. I was afraid if I had a partner he would get hurt. But I have to tell you, I learned my lesson: Supers working together are pretty powerful. If it hadn't been for my buddy Frozone and my family, none of us would be here to read this book. No joke.

⊕ Working Well with Others

My team is my family. My wife, Helen, is also known as Elastigirl. She can bend and stretch into almost any shape imaginable. She also can deck a villain from around a corner or down a city block. My son Dash is Super-fast. Violet, my daughter, can turn invisible *and* create force fields.

A Super Tip from MR. INCREDIBLE Don't work alone. It takes teamwork to save the world.

MR. iNCREDIBLE REMEMBERS:

A Lesson in Teamwork

Now, I'll admit that I didn't fully realize my family's skills until they actually rescued me from the island of Nomanisan. First Helen got me out of Syndrome's lair. Then we found Dash and Vi, and the four of us were fighting a jungle full of guards pretty well . . . until Syndrome showed up and zapped us all with his immobi-ray.

It was Vi who saved us. She used her force field to rock herself free. Then she simply walked over to Syndrome's control panel and turned off the immobi-ray. That's my girl!

After that, we were off to save the world from Syndrome. Once we made it to Metroville, where the Omnidroid was already on a rampage, I told my family to stay behind. I wanted to work alone. I didn't want anyone to get hurt.

That's when Helen set me straight. She convinced me that if we all worked together, we'd have a much better chance of beating Syndrome and his Omnidroid. She was right.

At first, Syndrome's evil plan worked.
The Omnidroid was loose, and Syndrome
looked like a hero fighting against it.
But he really was just controlling it with
his remote.

Then Syndrome ran into trouble. The
Omnidroid was smart enough to zap the
remote with a laser and then fire at
Syndrome's rocket boots. Now Syndrome
was down for the count. But the robot was
still on the loose!

When we arrived, the Omnidroid went
straight after Violet and Dash. Vi created
a force field to protect them. But then the

robot sat on the field and crushed it.
Luckily, I managed to save the kids just
in time.

Helen was in true Elastigirl form. And the
kids were . . . incredible! Then Frozone
arrived, and we became unbeatable. The
four of them got the remote control while I
struggled to point the Omnidroid's claw
back at its own body.

Helen pressed a button on the remote control that caused the claw to rocket down the street and smash right into the middle of the robot. The Omnidroid stood there with a gaping hole through its center. Out of commission, it fell over into the river and exploded.

Ka-boom!

And that, my friends, was the end of that.

A Super Tip from MR. INCREDIBLE Teamwork is great. When your team is your family, it's even better.

ⓘ Trusting Your Team

It's important to understand that you have to trust your teammates to do the right thing. You do your part, and they will do theirs.

Let me give you an example. When we returned home from defeating the Omnidroid, my son Jack-Jack had a new "babysitter." It was that dirty rotten Syndrome! We hardly had time to think. We just went into action.

Jack-Jack started to cry as Syndrome blasted a hole in the roof and used his rocket boots to fly up to his jet. Then Jack-Jack got angry. I don't know what the little guy did, but he took care of Syndrome on his own.

Syndrome dropped Jack-Jack in fear. Then he lost control of his rocket boots and started spinning wildly.

Jack-Jack plunged toward the ground. I threw Helen into the air. (That's the trust I'm talking about.) She managed to grab Jack-Jack and then bloom into a parachute so they could float safely to the ground.

Meanwhile, Syndrome recovered and got back on his jet. He was standing near the docking doors, screaming that he was still going to get my son. But I wasn't about to let that happen.

As much as I hated to do it, I reached over and chucked my brand-new sports car at Syndrome's jet. That knocked it off-kilter, and Syndrome started to slide toward the turbines. Unfortunately for him, he was wearing a cape. And I think we all remember from Chapter 5 what happens when capes meet turbines.

Ouch.

The jet exploded, hurling wreckage at us—but Vi put up a force field that saved the family. That was when I knew for sure: as long as we worked together, nothing could defeat us.

After all, we're Supers. What could happen?

A Super Tip from MR. INCREDIBLE Never underestimate the powers of your Super family.

Duty Calls!

Supers are back, but that doesn't mean the world is a completely safe place. There will always be villains out there, and it's up to you and me to try to stop them.

Being a Super has its perks, but it's a lot of responsibility. You never get to sleep late. Sometimes you just feel like saying, "What the heck—let that villain take over the world. I don't feel like saving everyone today." But it's important to always use your powers to help people, not just to show off or play pranks. (Did you hear that, Dash?)

Sure, it's great fun to be able to jump halfway across the state of Arkansas, or lift the corner of a skyscraper, or run faster than a rocket sled. But in the end, your Super powers will mean a whole lot more when you use them to save someone.

I hope you've found this book Super-helpful. And remember—if your powers fail you, and you find yourself without a backup team, it's really your wit and your grit that will make the difference. Never forget that.